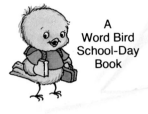

A
Word Bird
School-Day
Book

WORD BIRD'S
RAINY~DAY DANCE

by Jane Belk Moncure
illustrated by Linda Hohag
color by Lori Jacobson

Created by

THE
CHILD'S
WORLD

Distributed by CHILDRENS PRESS ®
Chicago, Illinois

CHILDRENS PRESS HARDCOVER EDITION
ISBN 0-516-06604-8

CHILDRENS PRESS PAPERBACK EDITION
ISBN 0-516-46604-6

Library of Congress Cataloging in Publication Data

Moncure, Jane Belk.
   Word Bird's rainy-day dance / by Jane Belk Moncure ; illustrated
by Linda Hohag.
      p. cm. — (A Word Bird school-day book)
   Summary: Animal students in school use a story dance to show how
seeds, sun, and rain combine to produce growing plants.
   ISBN 0-89565-579-9
   [1. Schools—Fiction.   2. Gardening—Fiction.   3. Dancing—
Fiction.   4. Animals—Fiction.   5. Vocabulary.]   I. Hohag, Linda
ill.   II. Title.   III. Series: Moncure, Jane Belk.   Word Bird school-
day book.
PZ7.M739Wop   1990
[E]—dc20
                                                    90-31693
                                                      CIP
                                                      AC

©1990 The Child's World, Inc.
Elgin, IL
All rights reserved. Printed in U.S.A.

1 2 3 4 5 6 7 8 9 10 11 12 R 99 98 97 96 95 94 93 92 91 90

WORD BIRD'S
RAINY~DAY DANCE

One rainy day Miss Beary said,
"Let's dance a rainy-day story
dance. Who wants to be a
farmer?"

"I do," said Word Bird. "I will be
the farmer in our dance."

"I will be a carrot," said Bunny.

"I will be an apple tree," said
Mouse.

"I will be a flower," said Cat.

"Now we need raindrops for the
story dance," said Word Bird.
"We will be raindrops," said
Frog and Duck.

"Are we ready?" asked Frog.
"Wait," said Word Bird. "We
need sunshine for our story
dance."

"I will be the sunshine," said
Pig. "I will do a sunshine
dance."

"The rest of us will be the wind,"
said Miss Beary. "We will blow
the raindrops."

Word Bird made a stage by
using blocks. Then he called
Bunny, Mouse, and Cat to the
stage.

"Here we go," said Word Bird.
"The farmer plows the ground
and plants seeds—one by one."

He gave Bunny, Mouse, and
Cat each a pat on the head,
and they curled up on the floor.

"The farmer rakes the ground,"
said Word Bird.
Bunny giggled. Mouse giggled
too.

"And he pulls the weeds," Word
Bird said.

Word Bird pulled Cat's tail, just
a tiny bit. Cat giggled. "I'm not
a weed," he said.

"Now it is our turn," said Frog
and Duck. "We are raindrops.
Drip-drop. Drip-drop."

Frog jumped over the little
seeds. "The rain is raining all
around," he sang.

"Splash !"

"It rains on the farmer's field,"
said Duck. "And it makes mud
puddles."

"The wind blows the raindrops,"
said Frog.
Everyone blew. And Frog nearly
fell over.

"The little seeds pop out of the ground," said Word Bird.
And Bunny, Mouse, and Cat popped up.

"It's my turn," said Pig. "The sun shines on the little plants." She danced on her toes until . . .

her big, yellow hat fell off and
rolled away. "Oh dear," she
said, running after it.

"Keep dancing," said Word
Bird.
Bunny stood up on her toes.

"Now I am a crunchy carrot, thanks to the rain and sun," she said.

"I am a little tree. I will keep growing until I will have big, juicy apples," said Mouse.
"And I am a flower, blowing in the wind," said Cat.

As the story dance came to an end, Word Bird said, "First came the raindrops, then came the sun . . .

and the little plants grew one
by one. The End."

"You did such a good story
dance," said Miss Beary. "I think
we will have . . .

a bubble party for a rainy-day
treat. Blow lots and lots of
bubbles." And everyone did.

You can read these words with
Word Bird.

rain

raindrops

sun

seed

carrot

apple

flower

wind

Frog

Duck

Pig

Bunny

Mouse

Cat